afterlife:
a ghost story

by Steve Yockey

A SAMUEL FRENCH ACTING EDITION

SAMUEL FRENCH

FOUNDED 1830

SAMUELFRENCH.COM

ISBN 978-0-573-70086-6   Printed in U.S.A.   #20466

MUSIC USE NOTE

IMPORTANT BILLING AND CREDIT
REQUIREMENTS

AFTERLIFE: A GHOST STORY was presented in workshop as a part of Southern Rep's New Play Bacchanal, January 21 – 24, 2010. It then opened in full production with support from the National New Play Network's Continued Life program on October 23, 2010 at Southern Rep in New Orleans, LA. The Artistic Director was Aimee Hayes and the Managing Director was Marieke Gaboury. The performance was directed by Aimee Hayes, with sets by Martin Andrew, costumes by Laura Sirkin-Brown, lights by Joan Long, sound by Mike Harkins, and puppets by Pandora Gastelum. The cast was as follows:

DANIELLE . . . . Lucy Faust

CONNOR . . . . Michael Aaron Santos

YOUNG MAN . . . . Andrew Farrier

POSTMAN/BLACKBIRD . . . . John Neisler

SEAMSTRESS . . . . Lisa Picone

PROPRIETRESS . . . . Troi Bechet

AFTERLIFE: A GHOST STORY opened with support from the National New Play Network's Continued Life program on January 17, 2011 at the Arsenal Center for the Arts' Charles Mosesian Theater in Watertown, MA. It was produced by New Repertory Theatre with Artistic Director Kate Warner and Managing Director Harriet Sheets. The performance was directed by Kate Warner, with sets by Cristina Todesco, costumes by Frances McSherry, lights by Karen Parsons, sound by David Remedios, and puppets by Pandora Gastelum. The cast was as follows:

DANIELLE . . . . Marianna Bassham

CONNOR . . . . Thomas Piper

YOUNG MAN . . . . Karl Baker Olson

POSTMAN/BLACKBIRD . . . . Dale Place

SEAMSTRESS . . . . Georgia Lyman

PROPRIETRESS . . . . Adrianne Krstansky

CHARACTERS

DANIELLE - a woman, thirties, a wife, with a sharp wit and wounded heart, unrecovered and angry but putting up a front, holding a grudge epic in both scale and focus

CONNOR - a man, thirties, a husband, attractive, affable, even charming; doing his best under the circumstances, but sorely mistaken in the belief that things are getting better

YOUNG MAN - a young man, late teens, optimistic, hopeful and brave, fueled by half-memories and things collected along the way; his clothes are worse for wear

THE PROPRIETRESS - a woman, effortlessly assured, precise, very neat and put together, hospitable running her teahouse, she is the ocean and means business

THE SEAMSTRESS - a woman, a raw nerve, taunting, mocking, a guest long past her welcome and unwilling to leave; rage, regret and laughter while wasting away

BLACK BIRD - a large, articulate bird, black feathers, warm and gentle in demeanor, seemingly playful but only as a means to an end; a functionary, a messenger

The **BLACK BIRD** *is a puppet operated by the actor playing the* **POSTMAN**. *See staging notes.*

POSTMAN - a letter carrier, someone who lives at sea, brusque but humane, in layers, a jacket & wool cap with a satchel; a functionary, a messenger

SETTING

ACT I

Takes place in and around a modern beach house in the shadow of an impending storm; it has warmth to it, somewhere people live. Home.

ACT II

The stage is radically altered into 3 spare playing areas demarcated by light and markings on the ground: the inside of a small cabin, a clearing among bare birch trees and a simply appointed teahouse.

AUTHOR'S NOTES

[ ] indicates overlapping dialogue.

The Black Bird is a large puppet. Although loosely inspired by Bunraku puppetry and operated by Postman, it will ideally be more of a Visible Means puppet and no effort should be made to disguise the operator. Closest to a giant crane in stature with black feathers, the head, elongated neck and one wing (or some representation of body) serve as the central expressive elements.

ACT I "OCEANIC MISFORTUNE"

i. the return

(Lights up on the living room of a house, well-appointed, simple and clean. It sits on the beach and belongs there. A couch, an end table with a lamp, a coffee table, a small bookshelf. A small group of assorted picture frames sits on top of the bookshelf. They are all empty.)

(Early evening. The sounds of the ocean waves are heard from outside.)

(DANIELLE stands in the open doorway, taking in the room. She is in jeans and an oversized sweater with a darker t-shirt underneath. She drops her small travel bag onto the ground; really, it just falls from her hand.)

CONNOR. How is it? Danielle?

(CONNOR enters with a duffle bag, pressing past her into the room. He's in khakis and some kind of polo shirt; dressed comfortably.)

DANIELLE. It looks fine.

CONNOR. Seems like everything's okay.

(He crosses into the back of the house. From offstage…)

Doesn't even feel like we were gone.

DANIELLE. No, it doesn't.

(DANIELLE takes a cautious step into the room. After a moment, CONNOR returns from deeper in the house. The bag is gone.)

CONNOR. I opened the windows in the bedroom to let some air in.

DANIELLE. Huh, until it starts raining.

CONNOR. It'll be okay.

DANIELLE. The furniture actually looks cleaner.

CONNOR. You think?

DANIELLE. I don't know, maybe. Are you going to check out back?

CONNOR. Yep, I'll do it now.

(He exits out to the beach. **DANIELLE** *moves to follow him, but looks out towards the ocean, sees it, then stops and moves back to the same place.* **CONNOR** *returns, looking over his shoulder…)*

The weather reports aren't wrong; the water is really churning. Looks like this storm is going to be a big one.

DANIELLE. Please, they always sound the alarms on the local weather; you know that. It's never as bad as they predict. We probably made the trip out here for nothing.

CONNOR. We needed to come back anyway, check [on things.]

DANIELLE. [It's when the] weather reports don't say anything, that's when it's the worst.

CONNOR. This time it looks like they're right.

DANIELLE. *(waving him off with a smirk…)* We'll see.

CONNOR. And, huh, there's, um…there's something else.

DANIELLE. Why are you making that face?

CONNOR. Okay, so, I don't know, but there are dead fish all over the beach.

DANIELLE. What are you talking about?

CONNOR. I don't, I'm not making it up, there are dead fish washed up on the beach, all different sizes. Look for yourself.

DANIELLE. I don't want to see that, why would I want to see that?

CONNOR. It's bizarre.

DANIELLE. Maybe they were trying to beat the storm too.

CONNOR. And there are these really big birds out [there too.]

DANIELLE. [Jesus,] Connor, do you work for *National Geographic* now? Enough with the nature reports; can we just focus on what we're here to do?

CONNOR. Very nice.

DANIELLE. I'm just, I'm ready to push up my sleeves and get to work.

CONNOR. So pick up your bag and come in already.

DANIELLE. Right. I don't even, let's get started.

(She shakes any remnants of hesitation off and enters the house.)

CONNOR. I'll go get the storm shutters out of storage if you wanna' unpack, but I'll need your help actually putting them up.

DANIELLE. I can do that. I think.

CONNOR. Never having done it, let's just both pretend it's gonna' be as easy as to get them up as I think.

DANIELLE. And I should check the kitchen.

CONNOR. What's wrong with the kitchen?

DANIELLE. No, check for food. For something to eat. We'll need to eat.

CONNOR. I'll run to that little market, what's [it called?]

DANIELLE. [I'm sure the] stores have been wiped out by now. Storm panic, everyone stocks up, everyone that's not leaving.

CONNOR. They'll still have something.

DANIELLE. Connor, I'm not going to battle for scraps at the store if we have perfectly good food in the kitchen.

CONNOR. Battle who? Did you even see anyone else?

DANIELLE. A few people, here and there when we were driving in.

CONNOR. Everyone's busy.

DANIELLE. Busy evacuating.

CONNOR. Point taken, we won't be here long.

DANIELLE. It's fine, I'll just make some soup or something.

CONNOR. Soup?

DANIELLE. That's what I said.

CONNOR. What kind of soup?

DANIELLE. Whatever kind of, who cares, do you care? Soup, just soup.

CONNOR. Hey, listen, soup sounds great.

DANIELLE. Good.

CONNOR. *(motioning towards the beach)* And maybe some fish too?

DANIELLE. Ugh. How long do you think this is all going to take?

CONNOR. Okay, well, we probably won't have much time tonight, but we'll get a lot done by tomorrow I think. Tomorrow afternoon at the latest. I mean, we have to finish before the storm rolls in or what's the point?

DANIELLE. What's the point of any of it?

CONNOR. We just got here.

DANIELLE. Uh huh.

CONNOR. Let's not, okay?

DANIELLE. I'm not. But…maybe we should have waited.

CONNOR. Don't do that, you said you were worried about the house, too. And you were going nuts in my parents' guest room.

DANIELLE. I think a hotel would have been fine, if we needed to leave your parents' house.

CONNOR. Okay, first off, you hate hotels.

DANIELLE. I hate…aspects of hotels.

CONNOR. You've never enjoyed a hotel we've stayed at, ever, not once. Uh uh, not once. And we shouldn't be living in a hotel anyway. Or in a tiny guest room. And that's what we were starting to do, live there. But we have a house right here. We've been [away…]

DANIELLE. *(victoriously)* [Ha! I knew] you wanted to come back. Not just because of [the storm.]

CONNOR. [We decided] to come back. Second off, what if the storm turns out to be as awful as they're saying and we didn't close everything up? Do you want to replace every window? Besides you were as anxious to get back here as I was, so change your mind if you want but at least acknowledge that's what you're doing.

DANIELLE. All right, fine. But I didn't want to get back here, just away from there. I couldn't take any more of your family. Or my family, my family too. Any family. The funeral happened and then time just passed and passed and [passed.]

CONNOR. [Got it.]

DANIELLE. The storm is just a convenient excuse.

CONNOR. We'll see how convenient it turns out to be once [it's over.]

DANIELLE. [Oh, you] know what [I mean.]

CONNOR. [Look, I know] it's not, all of those people, they love us. And maybe, and I'm saying maybe, all right, maybe I needed to get away as much as you did, but they're just trying to help.

DANIELLE. Well, they can't help.

CONNOR. They don't know what to do.

DANIELLE. Huh, neither do we. *(She catches herself and shakes it off.)* But I'm fine, this is fine.

CONNOR. There's not a road map for any of this, right? I just, I put away all of the pictures before we left, packed up his things, so let's just try not to dwell on it.

*(**DANIELLE** laughs, but it's not funny, while somehow signaling for him to stop.)*

DANIELLE. Listen to you.

CONNOR. I don't know what to tell you, Danielle, we had to come back eventually.

DANIELLE. Did we?

(pause)

CONNOR. So…you're gonna' make soup?

DANIELLE. I don't even know.

CONNOR. Well I'm gonna' go and, go get the storm shutters.

DANIELLE. Right.

CONNOR. Will you call your folks and let them know we're here?

DANIELLE. Ugh, I know how this sounds, but I really, really don't want to.

CONNOR. Danielle.

DANIELLE. My mom's going to ask, "How was the drive?" But that's not what she means, she means, "How are you feeling?" Because everything she says to me now means, "How are you feeling?"

CONNOR. It doesn't have to be a long call.

DANIELLE. Fine.

(He begins to exit as she picks up the phone.)

No dial tone.

CONNOR. Ah fuck, I forgot, I shut it off.

DANIELLE. Why?

CONNOR. I didn't know how long we'd be gone.

DANIELLE. Long. So it looks like I can't call them. Too bad.

(She very deliberately places the receiver back down on the phone.)

CONNOR. You don't seem disappointed.

DANIELLE. Ya' know, I'd call them if I could.

CONNOR. Fine, I'll take care of it.

DANIELLE. No doubt.

CONNOR. After the weather passes.

DANIELLE. Yep, post-evacuation.

CONNOR. Sure.

DANIELLE. You'll take care of everything.

CONNOR. Jesus, are you trying to pick a fight? That's a stupid question, it's pretty clear that's what you're doing, just tell me what the fight's about so we can get to it.

(She lets out a quick laugh, it's a sharp thing, an exhalation.)

DANIELLE. We're not going to fight, Connor; we don't fight anymore.

CONNOR. What does that even mean?

DANIELLE. It means that you'll back down rather than push me because you're so fucking chipper and I'm so fucking fragile that everyone has to walk on tiptoe all the time. And then they try to pretend that they're not walking on tiptoe and don't make that face at me because you know damn well that's what you do, and that's why we don't fight anymore, and that's why we're not in this house anymore.

(pause)

CONNOR. Okay.

DANIELLE. Like that, you're doing it right now.

CONNOR. Doing what?

DANIELLE. Pacifying.

CONNOR. No, I'm not. And look, it's not easy for me coming back here either.

DANIELLE. I know.

CONNOR. Do you?

DANIELLE. Yes, I just…I'm sorry.

CONNOR. You don't have to apologize. And I'm not tiptoeing, or I'm not trying to tiptoe, or however it won't sound patronizing. Because I'm not. Let's just get everything done that needs to get done and we can leave.

DANIELLE. Right.

CONNOR. We'll be gone before the storm gets too bad and then we'll just wait and see.

DANIELLE. That's…a plan.

CONNOR. That's a good plan.

DANIELLE. Sure.

CONNOR. Just give me tonight and tomorrow. We're figuring out how to do this thing, we're each figuring it out. But we have to let ourselves, right?

DANIELLE. It's just being here. That's all it is. I didn't think it would be, not all, like it's hanging in the air.

CONNOR. It's still home.

DANIELLE. I'm fine. Really.

CONNOR. It's okay, you don't have to keep saying [it.]

DANIELLE. [You] should get started.

CONNOR. I'll come and grab you in a little bit when I need your help.

DANIELLE. Mm hm, and then I'll help.

(He kisses her on the cheek and exits. She begins to cry, or just lose control, but just as quickly she stops herself.)

END SCENE

ii. the beach again

(On the beach. The next morning. Almost dawn, the sound of waves, soft and dull. More present now.)

(DANIELLE sits with the same large sweater pulled over her knees. She is barefoot.)

(Next to her, a trail of smoke snakes from the remnants of a driftwood bonfire.)

(She stares out at the ocean. The sun rises. For a moment the brilliance of the dawning light brightens DANIELLE's eyes, lifting her a bit. It is a beautiful moment. Just as quickly the moment passes.)

(CONNOR enters, yawning. He is barefoot, in pajama pants and a t-shirt. He has a mug.)

CONNOR. Hey.

DANIELLE. You missed the sunrise, the pretty part.

CONNOR. Have you been out here all night?

DANIELLE. Most of the night.

CONNOR. I saw you started packing up some things.

DANIELLE. I tried a little, but I couldn't really focus. We're just going back to your parents' house, right? I don't know what to "save" from the big scary storm.

CONNOR. Anything you can't live without, just in case.

DANIELLE. Not much to pack.

CONNOR. I love how cavalier you're being about this entire, ugh, okay, what is that smell?

DANIELLE. And I cleared away a bunch of the fish.

CONNOR. *(looking around)* Huh.

DANIELLE. They were starting to rot and I didn't want to look at them. So I burned them.

CONNOR. What?

DANIELLE. I collected them up and I burned them in the bonfire. Don't make that face, what was I supposed to do, throw them back in the ocean?

CONNOR. So you burned them, no, that makes perfect sense.

DANIELLE. Well, that's what I did.

CONNOR. No one could ever build a bonfire like you. And I'm betting no one's ever built one like that, huh, dead fish bonfire.

DANIELLE. It was dark out here and quiet, except for the waves. Then I heard some kind of, I heard, I don't know, I just needed to do something; I couldn't sleep.

CONNOR. Me either.

DANIELLE. I thought you were out cold.

CONNOR. Eh, for a while, kind of, but then it was more up and down, you know? All these things in my, all the things we need to get done before we head out, just things.

DANIELLE. We should do the storm shutters this morning, you think? Just go ahead and get it out of the way.

CONNOR. We can do that, sure. Anyway, last night I ended up walking the beach a little.

DANIELLE. You were out here? Did you, did you see the fire?

CONNOR. Well I was farther down the beach, but I saw it. Saw you. I just thought maybe you wanted some time to yourself out here.

DANIELLE. Did you?

CONNOR. It's windier, huh?

DANIELLE. No rain yet, but I think maybe you can see it in the clouds.

CONNOR. It's coming.

DANIELLE. Or so the ominous weather report tells us.

CONNOR. You just said you could see it in the clouds.

DANIELLE. I did say that.

CONNOR. You won't be disappointed, Danielle, there's gonna' be a storm.

DANIELLE. Right here, it looks different now, doesn't it? The shape of the beach; the water seems closer. That sounds so strange, I guess.

CONNOR. It's something, how the shore line changes. I don't even feel like we've been gone that long, but when you're not looking at it every day it's like it all of the sudden shifts or moves, [or just...]

DANIELLE. [It's] washing away.

CONNOR. But there's something else, right? Something about looking at what's left.

(He waits. She gives nothing.)

Chilly this morning, you want a blanket?

DANIELLE. The sweater's warm.

CONNOR. You could probably get the fire started again. It wouldn't [take long.]

DANIELLE. [The sun's] up, it'll be fine. You're still trying to take care of me.

CONNOR. I'm not doing it on purpose. Let's, we'll talk about something else. Oh, I saw another one of those big black birds. It was just standing in the surf.

DANIELLE. Where the hell did they even come from?

CONNOR. It looked almost like a statue. They'd be beautiful, maybe, if they weren't so loud.

DANIELLE. You can definitely hear them.

CONNOR. I think they're here because of all the dead fish.

DANIELLE. Great.

CONNOR. It's not something I would have even thought about. Dead fish.

(She chuckles.)

DANIELLE. Why would you, it's disgusting.

CONNOR. There's a little smile.

DANIELLE. Ugh. Let's just sit here and enjoy this not so terrible morning.

CONNOR. It's even a little nice.

DANIELLE. Something like nice.

CONNOR. While you stare down the ocean.

DANIELLE. I'm, I'm not staring down the ocean.

CONNOR. Uh huh, out here all night. It's only water, [Danielle.]

DANIELLE. [That's not] what I'm [doing.]

CONNOR. [You don't] want to own up to it, that's fine by me.

DANIELLE. I'm just having a, one of those déjà vu things. I don't know.

CONNOR. Sure. We used to spend so much time out here, huh?

DANIELLE. We did.

CONNOR. It instantly feels, it always felt so familiar.

DANIELLE. We practically lived out here.

CONNOR. That's why people move to the beach, right?

DANIELLE. To be at the beach.

CONNOR. To be at the beach.

DANIELLE. I loved living here.

CONNOR. It's a great place.

DANIELLE. Making bonfires at night, clear nights. And you bought those crazy blue mosquito lamps that were so complicated.

CONNOR. They were supposed to come with instructions.

DANIELLE. And they didn't even work.

CONNOR. Nope.

DANIELLE. Not at all.

CONNOR. And we took those walks, collecting little shells, rocks and building sandcastle after sandcastle [in the…]

DANIELLE. [Oh, with] all of his little plastic tools and that little bucket.

(Pause. They both look out at the water.)

Everything tiny, little shovel, smaller to fit his hands.

CONNOR. Hadn't thought about that in a while.

DANIELLE. Me either.

CONNOR. He was a good little guy.

DANIELLE. So little.

CONNOR. And it's so big out there.

DANIELLE. And we get dead fish.

CONNOR. I'd rather think about the sandcastles.

(She shakes it off and looks at him. He continues to look out at the water.)

DANIELLE. We did spend a lot of time out here.

CONNOR. I love you.

DANIELLE. I'm trying really hard to not let all of this...

(He looks at her. After a moment, she kisses him gently on the cheek with all of the tenderness that two people can share. He tears up but smiles at her.)

CONNOR. It's okay that it's hard.

DANIELLE. I love you too.

CONNOR. You want some of this?

DANIELLE. What is it?

CONNOR. Coffee. And some whiskey.

DANIELLE. *(laughing)* Perfect.

CONNOR. I know, it's early. But I [thought...]

DANIELLE. [I don't want] any.

CONNOR. Suit yourself.

*(He takes a drink, places his arm around **DANIELLE** and looks out into the sun.)*

Shame about the sunrise, I bet it was beautiful.

END SCENE

iii. in the waves

(The living room. Later the same day. The sound of the ocean waves can be heard, perhaps wind. The storm is getting closer.)

*(***DANIELLE*** *is still wearing the oversized sweater. She has one sealed packing box nearby and is placing books from a shelf into another open box.)*

(Quietly, a sigh rises out of the waves, breathy, choppy, almost inaudible. ***DANIELLE*** *stops and goes to the window to look out at the water. She listens, but there is only the sound of waves. She shakes it off.)*

*(***DANIELLE*** *returns to the packing box, but another sound rises out of the waves, a higher pitch this time, more of a voice and a bit more audible but still just an idea of a noise buried in the rhythmic sounds of the ocean. She freezes and turns to look out at the water again. She suddenly looks at the books in her hands, examines the room, looks at the empty picture frames and then violently hurls the books to the floor.)*

(She examines this, moves over to the couch, takes one of the pillows and tosses it to the ground. Suddenly in a burst, she knocks all of the pillows and cushions to the ground. She then knocks over another chair and tips over the coffee table rather violently.)

(Breathing heavy and undone, she examines this.)

*(***CONNOR*** *enters from the back of the house, now dressed, with his duffle bag and one or two other bags or suitcases.)*

CONNOR. What the fuck?

DANIELLE. Oh, I was just, I was trying to, to…

CONNOR. What?

DANIELLE. Move the couch. But it's too heavy.

CONNOR. Why?

DANIELLE. Just to see if, Jesus, it's no big deal. I just thought it might look better over…I don't know.

CONNOR. *(laughing it off)* Well, ask for help or something.

DANIELLE. I called out for you.

CONNOR. Uh huh, you never ask for help. Where do you want to move it?

DANIELLE. No, no it's fine. I changed my mind.

CONNOR. Okay.

DANIELLE. I was just cleaning this up.

*(**CONNOR** begins to restore the living room. **DANIELLE** watches the room return to order as he speaks.)*

CONNOR. So I walked through town this morning. Pretty quiet. Bought some coffee at that little place over on Oceanside. It was practically empty.

DANIELLE. That place is always crowded.

CONNOR. Not today.

DANIELLE. No, not today.

CONNOR. I guess people are probably off doing what we're doing, packing and closing up. Or already gone. Not the best time to have a chat or… *(He stops.)* Are you gonna' help?

DANIELLE. Oh, oh yes.

(She helps him set the coffee table upright.)

CONNOR. That's the point of evacuating I guess.

DANIELLE. Except for us. We charge right into the middle of it.

CONNOR. We'll be out of here soon.

DANIELLE. I don't think I've ever liked these pillows. I don't think I ever really even looked at these pillows.

CONNOR. They're fine.

DANIELLE. They go with the couch anyway.

CONNOR. You picked out everything in this place.

DANIELLE. I'm just making an observation Connor, I'm just saying out loud that they fit with everything but I'm not sure I particularly like them.

(The room is restored.)

CONNOR. There, exactly as before.

DANIELLE. Thanks.

CONNOR. Exactly as it was before whatever happened in here while I was back there.

DANIELLE. What does that [mean?]

CONNOR. [Hey, hey, hey,] I wasn't trying to start anything. I too was just, ya' know, making an observation. I'm sorry.

DANIELLE. Okay.

CONNOR. Everything's so tense.

DANIELLE. You mean I'm so tense.

CONNOR. No, I mean everything.

DANIELLE. Huh.

CONNOR. Isn't it?

DANIELLE. Yes.

CONNOR. I keep catching myself grinding my teeth.

DANIELLE. You do it in your sleep too. I can hear it.

CONNOR. You can?

DANIELLE. Like someone rubbing rocks together.

CONNOR. For how long?

DANIELLE. A while.

CONNOR. My jaw is starting to ache.

DANIELLE. Well, we've never faced down a natural disaster.

CONNOR. That's fair.

DANIELLE. And…we weren't really talking that much before the storm. It's hard to start talking again when you get used to not talking.

CONNOR. That's…fair.

(long pause)

DANIELLE. Is there, ugh, I have no idea why this is so hard, why is this so hard? Is there anything you want to say to me? I know how that, but just, is there [anything?]

CONNOR. [Yes.]

DANIELLE. Okay?

CONNOR. But you don't want to hear it.

DANIELLE. Yes I do. I think.

CONNOR. Just, look, can we take ten minutes to go for a walk, just around the [block or...?]

DANIELLE. [That's what] I don't want to hear?

CONNOR. Because you've only been in here, in the house, mostly in this room.

DANIELLE. I'm supposed to be packing things from in here.

CONNOR. It's two boxes of stuff Danielle, we're not taking everything. And I think maybe you're going a little stir crazy.

DANIELLE. I've been outside; I went to the beach.

CONNOR. I can't get you into town, you haven't talked to anyone.

DANIELLE. There's no one left around to [talk to.]

CONNOR. [Yes there] is and that's not the point.

DANIELLE. This isn't a social visit, get in and get out, you said that.

CONNOR. But I thought once we were here that you [would...]

DANIELLE. [What?]

CONNOR. Somehow, kind of...re-engage.

DANIELLE. You thought boarding up the house so it doesn't get washed away by a huge storm was a healthy way for me to re-enter our life?

CONNOR. Not when you say it like that. But this is home, this is where we lived and if it doesn't get washed away then this is where we'll be living again.

DANIELLE. All right, I'm starting to, the distance between our purpose here now, our task, and your expectations of me is unfathomable, isn't it? Do you feel that at all?

CONNOR. Look, I'll just, you say you're doing better, handling things, you "act" like you're doing better, but you're bad at it. I don't know if you think you're good at it, but you're not. Then I have to act like you are, and I was doing okay with that, but then we walk in this house and I can't act like I think you're okay anymore because you're clearly not.

DANIELLE. Well I thought I would be fine and I'm dealing with it so just let me deal with it.

CONNOR. I think that, I don't know, I was out on the beach alone [and...]

DANIELLE. [I thought] you were in town?

CONNOR. And then I went to the beach.

DANIELLE. Why?

CONNOR. It doesn't matter why. And the waves are really high, the wind's picking up. I think we should just go.

DANIELLE. You went to the beach and now you want to leave?

CONNOR. You asked me to tell you what I'm thinking, if I had anything [to...]

DANIELLE. [What] about closing up the house?

CONNOR. Okay, let's take some time to get things settled up and then [we can...]

DANIELLE. [Now you] want to stay?

CONNOR. I don't know, I don't know, Danielle. I don't want to flip over furniture and burn dead fish, I know that much; what do you think we should do?

DANIELLE. I don't want you to be angry with me.

CONNOR. I'm not angry. I'm just frustrated.

DANIELLE. No, when I say this, I don't want you to be angry with me.

CONNOR. What?

DANIELLE. Don't get angry.

CONNOR. Look, I know it must seem [like I'm...]

DANIELLE. *(in a sudden burst)* [I just, I] keep seeing it, he's there one second and then just gone, smiling, waving, showing off with those bright orange water wings [and then...]

CONNOR. [Why would] you, we said we wouldn't talk about it.

DANIELLE. We agreed to not talk about everything. Everything.

CONNOR. Stop it.

DANIELLE. This is what you wanted, right? I'm engaging you.

CONNOR. Okay, I'll stop it.

DANIELLE. We can't really get better if we just skim over things, it would look like we were touching them if someone was looking from far away, but we're not far away, we're right here and that's why we don't talk. We didn't even talk about it at his funeral. That's how much we haven't talked [about it.]

CONNOR. [Because it's] too hard to be back here when you're clearly not ready to come back here, even though you said you were, and I'm not even sure I'm ready, to have to look at the water every day.

DANIELLE. I know.

CONNOR. We said we wouldn't talk about it because we each needed to do our own thing, because we can't do it together, for whatever reason, and I've respected that.

DANIELLE. I know.

CONNOR. So you should respect it too.

DANIELLE. I know.

CONNOR. Stop saying "I know." Stop saying that. And don't cry.

DANIELLE. No, I'm not.

(She's not. He's close.)

CONNOR. I'm not going to, so you can't.

(She's stone.)

DANIELLE. All right. But it hasn't been that long. Not that long at all, not in the, and how long is long enough anyway? You can't just make something the past by saying we're getting past it, no matter how many times you say it. And when something like this happens, when that ocean gets hungry again and comes back for more, how [can we…]

CONNOR. [That's not] what's [happening.]

DANIELLE. [That ocean,] that fucking ocean [is awful.]

CONNOR. [Now we're] talking about the [ocean?]

DANIELLE. [I heard] him crying last night.

CONNOR. Who?

DANIELLE. No. *(Pause. She turns to him.)* I wasn't going to tell [you.]

CONNOR. [Are you] talking about…?

(pause)

Okay, listen, I didn't want to tell you this, but I don't know how to not tell you if you're going to stand there and…

*(**CONNOR** takes **DANIELLE** by the hand and sits her on the couch.)*

DANIELLE. What are you [doing?]

CONNOR. [Listen, I] have to, I've made my peace with it. That he's gone, figured out how to keep going, maybe it's not what you want, maybe that's difficult, but it's the best I can do and I did it.

*(For a moment, **DANIELLE** is stunned in a terrible kind of awe.)*

DANIELLE. What?

CONNOR. It's done. I'm done with it enough to try [to get…]

DANIELLE. [How?]

CONNOR. I don't know, it just [happened.]

DANIELLE. [Tell me how. I] don't know how, look at me.

CONNOR. It's gonna' sound… I took everything I feel about, I took everything I had to say, to him, put it in a letter and threw it in the ocean. The same place where he was washed out, just out there, right on the beach.

DANIELLE. A letter?

CONNOR. Yes.

DANIELLE. A letter is how you got over the death of our son?

CONNOR. Don't do that.

DANIELLE. What did it say?

CONNOR. It's between him and me. I'm sorry, I can't tell you. I know that's not fair, but it's only for him, with him and he's gone.

DANIELLE. A letter?

CONNOR. A letter.

DANIELLE. A fucking letter?

CONNOR. Goddamn it, [Danielle.]

DANIELLE. [Well I'm,] I'm glad you can make it better like that, but I can't. I heard a little boy crying last night, on the beach, and I think, I thought it [was...]

CONNOR. [Don't say] his name.

DANIELLE. We won't even say his name!

CONNOR. I can't, not yet.

DANIELLE. But you're healed now; you threw a letter in the ocean.

CONNOR. Cut away at me all you need to Danielle, if that's what [you need.]

DANIELLE. [I'm fucking] angry!

CONNOR. At least you're not pretending you're fine [anymore.]

DANIELLE. [You keep] saying pretending, I wasn't pretending to do [anything.]

CONNOR. [Oh no?]

DANIELLE. I was trying.

CONNOR. Try harder.

DANIELLE. We should be able to lean on each other and we found out we can't. Clearly that's a fucking disappointment, even still it doesn't mean I don't love you, but how can I talk to you when I actually see you recovering, when you're standing here presenting me with these "facts" and even the idea of recovering is still so menacingly foreign to me.

CONNOR. I understand.

DANIELLE. No you don't.

CONNOR. Okay, I don't.

DANIELLE. And we're back here now and all I can do is think about that ocean, it's all I can hear, it's always there, right there, and then his little voice calling for help like he might be just behind the next [wave.]

CONNOR. [I know you] think I'm being cruel, no, I think I'm being cruel but I've tried being everything else so listen: I love you and I will not watch you drive yourself crazy here; he's dead. He's dead. And this is the worst kind of [wallowing in…]

DANIELLE. [You know what] I was doing? On the beach?

CONNOR. No, I don't [really want…]

DANIELLE. [You had your] letter story, this is what I did: I built that fire last night and sat in the dark and I heard him, even though that's impossible and I don't care how it sounds and then it seemed like everything bent around me and stopped and all I could see were dead fish, can you imagine that moment? By firelight, dead fish everywhere, that ocean and the sound of my son [crying?]

CONNOR. [Okay, I] have to get out of here.

(He is up and heading for the door.)

DANIELLE. Where are you going?

CONNOR. I don't know. The beach, I don't [know.]

DANIELLE. [I'm sorry.]

CONNOR. You heard the wind.

DANIELLE. No, you're not [listening…]

CONNOR. [The wind!] And rain. It's ridiculous, Danielle. Our boy wasn't even, he was three years old and he will never have to cry again; we don't get to make it better, to do a better job. It couldn't have been him because he never gets to cry now.

DANIELLE. Stop.

CONNOR. But you wanted to talk [so badly.]

DANIELLE. [You wanted] to talk!

CONNOR. About getting past this!

DANIELLE. I know what I heard out [there.]

CONNOR. [I don't give] a damn what you think you heard. He disappeared right into the surf, right out of our hands, and you think the ocean wants more?

DANIELLE. That goddamn ocean can't have anymore.

CONNOR. It doesn't want anything; it's just [water.]

DANIELLE. [No! That] ocean took our son!

CONNOR. We live here, we chose this, we brought him here, isn't it nice on the beach? And we're so small compared to that, all [of that.]

DANIELLE. [What are] you, so it's our fault?

CONNOR. Terrible things just happen, Danielle.

DANIELLE. Terrible things just happen?

CONNOR. We're leaving tonight; I don't give a fuck about the house. We're leaving.

DANIELLE. On the beach, in the dark, he was crying.

CONNOR. We cry. That's something we do. And that's it.

(He exits.)

END SCENE

iv. sinking hearts

(The beach again. Early evening. The sound of waves, louder, more forceful. Alive. The sky is grayer and moving with the impending storm.)

(DANIELLE sits with the same large sweater pulled over her knees. She is barefoot.)

DANIELLE. You're not fooling anyone, you know? Well, you're not fooling me. You're a false neighbor. Maybe something I should have expected. Am I naïve? To be fair, I'm not fooling anyone either. I wasn't fooling anyone, but the secret is really out now. Connor's packing the car. I should be trying to help, trying to talk to him. Trying to apologize. Jesus, we never even put up the storm shutters. Huh, but instead of anywhere else, here I am. And just look at me. And just look at you.

You know, since you took our son, my son, I think my heart actually pumps slower. Like it takes more for it to keep going. Like I have to really try when it used to be so effortless. Honestly, it feels like it would be easier to just give in than keep overcoming the pain of every beat, every beat that sends blood rushing out to find, when it reaches my eyes, my hands in this fucking sand, that I'm still alone. Even with Connor, I'm alone. All I have here are memories that I can't enjoy ever again and you: a vast, never-ending gravesite. Aren't you pretty? But we're not so different, you and me. Wave after wave after wave thrown against the shore, the same motion over and over again, clawing at the beach like each time you might get a solid grip. And instead, slowly over time, you just drag everything away. Out there. In here. *(She points to her head.)* And in here. *(She touches her chest.)* I do that too, the same feelings, the same thoughts, over and over. I want him back. I hate you. I want him back. I hate you. You think maybe we do it because we don't know how to do anything else, like something inside is truly broken but keeps trying to finish anyway?

Honestly, it's not just you and me though, I guess. There's Connor, poor well-meaning, "recovering" Connor. That's not fair. And there's all of our family who don't know me anymore, how could they know me? They can't see me anymore. I can't see me anymore. All I can see is you. And I do see you. I fucking see you now, the real you, so hungry and large. How could I ever have trusted something that does nothing but take? Do you have him out there somewhere? Holding him tight so he can't come home. I should let you take me, too. Would you like that? Do you want that? Let you reach in through my mouth and pull everything out it one motion so I just buckle and collapse, my lungs, my heart, all of it. I would give you all of it if you'd just take these memories, too. *(She stands up.)* We lived next to you for years and you just couldn't resist, could you? He was a beautiful boy and you wanted him. So you took him because you get what you want, right? You're a beast. And I do hate you. I hate you. I hate you! I hate…

(Lightning crashes causing **DANIELLE** *to leap a bit.)*

Fucking ocean.

END SCENE

v. death

(The living room. Just a bit later. But a single lamp provides the light as the storm rages outside, dark and menacing.)

*(***CONNOR*** charges through the door speaking, soaking wet, stripping drenched clothing from his body. He has red claw marks down his neck and the top of his chest.)*

*(***DANIELLE*** follows him through the door, a bit slower. She is also soaking wet.)*

CONNOR. Jesus Danielle, you could have fucking drowned, you [could've…]

DANIELLE. [I just need] to warm up.

CONNOR. Because I happened to see you, in all that chop, because I fucking swam out there to get you, what were you doing?

DANIELLE. I don't know, [I just…]

CONNOR. [And you] know, it felt like you were trying to pull me under. I don't know, fuck.

(pause)

Fucking say something!

DANIELLE. Stop yelling, I'm fine.

CONNOR. Okay, okay no, fucking tell me what is going through your head when you swim out in the middle of that?!

DANIELLE. I thought I saw…something. I thought I saw something out in the [water.]

CONNOR. [What?]

DANIELLE. Are you okay?

CONNOR. No.

DANIELLE. I didn't mean to go out so far.

CONNOR. You didn't mean to, huh, you just decided to go swimming, in the ocean, with a storm coming in, a huge storm. I'm packing the car, I turn around and you're gone?

DANIELLE. I couldn't [leave yet.]

CONNOR. [It's crazy out] there, we were getting tossed around out there; we could have died out there. I know you're sad, but Jesus [fucking...]

DANIELLE. [You're] bleeding.

CONNOR. What?

DANIELLE. Connor, you're bleeding.

(He examines his neck and chest in the mirror.)

CONNOR. You took a huge chunk out of my neck, look at this, it's [so deep.]

DANIELLE. [I'll get] some towels.

CONNOR. Just, just rest. I'll go.

(He exits. The storm gets louder.)

DANIELLE. I didn't just go swimming.

CONNOR. I can't hear you.

DANIELLE. *(louder)* I didn't just go swimming.

CONNOR. You need to dry off before you get sick.

DANIELLE. I thought I saw someone out in the water. I didn't know what to do. I didn't want to just get in the car and drive [away if...]

(CONNOR enters shirtless with a towel over his shoulders, also holding some additional towels.)

CONNOR. [There was] no one out there.

DANIELLE. I was trying to help.

CONNOR. There was no one out there.

DANIELLE. There was, I saw [him.]

CONNOR. [Well then] whoever you saw is at the bottom of the ocean now.

(She slaps him.)

What the fuck?

DANIELLE. I'm sorry, I don't, I'm sorry.

CONNOR. You're not, you're not even a good swimmer. What made you think you [could...?]

DANIELLE. [I didn't] think about it, I just ran into the water.

CONNOR. Take these.

(He hands her the towels and sits down. The storm is louder.)

We have to get out of here.

DANIELLE. How's your neck?

CONNOR. It'll be okay.

DANIELLE. You surprised me, it was just a reaction, it wasn't, I got so turned around and I couldn't see the shore.

(She moves over to him leaving the towel behind and gently touches the scratch marks. **CONNOR** *winces but doesn't stop her. A crash of lightning and thunder punctuates a flicker of electricity in the house.)*

There's something going on with me.

CONNOR. I know.

DANIELLE. It's not a normal something. And I can't leave.

CONNOR. We don't have time for this [right now.]

DANIELLE. [I don't] know what to do.

CONNOR. Put some dry clothes on. We have to go.

DANIELLE. Connor, I saw him in the water. I heard him on the beach last night and then today, I saw him out in the waves.

(Another crack of thunder. The lights flicker sporadically and lightning flashes from the storm brighten the room. A rumbling noise begins to grow. It continues to grow through the rest of the scene, the sound of water moving, massing. **CONNOR** *pushes her away. And gets up.)*

CONNOR. Where are my clothes?

DANIELLE. It shouldn't be real, but it [was real.]

CONNOR. [Had to wait] until we put everything in [the car.]

DANIELLE. [I'm not] leaving him again.

CONNOR. We didn't leave him, [Danielle.]

DANIELLE. [He's out] there. We didn't ever find him, not his body, so you don't know, for Christ sake we buried an empty box! He's out [there and...]

CONNOR. [His body might] be out there, somewhere, but he's not, not in a way that he's ever coming [back.]

DANIELLE. [But how] do you know that? How [do you...?]

CONNOR. [Jesus Christ,] you could be dead, do you get that [at all?]

DANIELLE. [Yes.]

CONNOR. Yes!

DANIELLE. Yes!! And I don't care, I don't know what else to say, I don't care, I don't care! I don't want to be alive if he's not with me, I know people get over these things, but not all people because I can't, and I wanted it to be gone, all of it, everything, everything, you and me, all of the memories of a little boy whose name I don't want to remember. How sick is that?

(The storm is battering the house.)

CONNOR. You're going to be okay, it [does get better.]

DANIELLE. [That's just] some awful lie people tell [themselves.]

CONNOR. [It has to] get better.

DANIELLE. Why?! Why does it have to get [better?]

CONNOR. [Because] it can't be like this!

*(**DANIELLE** suddenly starts laughing; it's almost frightening.)*

DANIELLE. He's still in the water.

CONNOR. We shouldn't have come back. I had no idea [you would...]

DANIELLE. [Don't you see, we] had to come back for him!

*(**CONNOR** grabs **DANIELLE** by the arm.)*

CONNOR. Look at me; let's get out of [here.]

DANIELLE. [I will] not leave him.

CONNOR. I can make [you leave.]

(She explodes away from him.)

DANIELLE. [I thought I might] drown, I really did, before you pulled me out and I can't even begin to explain the feeling in my heart, the kind of lifting, like I was being pulled up, not down, up by some huge hook right through my chest, up into the sky, like floating above everything, like anything was possible, like I might see him again at any moment, it felt so good and, and then you pulled me back to shore, like someone ripped the hook right out and everything I thought might happen spilled out onto this impossibly clean rug, how can the rug be so fucking clean? How can the house still be so clean?! We're not! And how can that fucking ocean sit there so smugly, like some great, untouchable [thing?]

(As **DANIELLE** *continues,* **CONNOR** *slowly crosses towards the windows that face the beach. His eyes go wide.)*

CONNOR. [Oh my] [god.]

DANIELLE. [I know] you're getting better, I'm not. I know you're going to be all right, but I hate it, none of it should be here, not without him, none [of it.]

CONNOR. [Danielle!] Look, look!!

(They look out the window as the roar of the water becomes deafening. For a moment, they are both still with shock.)

DANIELLE. What is that?

(He grabs her by the hand and tries to drag her towards the door as she screams and fights against him, knocking over furniture, reaching towards the windows.)

CONNOR. We have, we have to go [now!]

DANIELLE. [What] is that?!

CONNOR. Danielle, [let's go!]

DANIELLE. [We've got] to save him! Look at that thing! [Look at it!]

CONNOR. [We have to] go. Stop it, [we have to...]

DANIELLE. [Give him] back!!

(Blackout as the sounds of **DANIELLE** *and* **CONNOR** *struggling are drowned out by waves crashing down on the house. The sounds of lumber snapping, smashing and glass breaking consume the stage. The sounds of a lifetime being swallowed, consumed. The sounds of a lifetime being erased.)*

END OF ACT

ACT II "AFTER LIFE"

i. epistolary

(The interior of a small, weathered cottage.)

*(A **YOUNG MAN** stands alone. He holds a piece of paper in one hand and an envelope in the other. He wears a pair of worn pants and a thin, striped, weathered sweater. His feet are bare and dirty. But he has an undeniable air of optimism.)*

(There is a single, straight-back chair. A large pile of shredded paper, torn up envelopes and unsent mail has collected nearby.)

YOUNG MAN. Dear Mom and Dad,

How are you? I've grown so quickly, even since my last letter. I wish you could see. I'm sad to say I don't know exactly where I am and it's proving so difficult to get back. The weather is keeping me away for now; the ocean looks angry. I'm not able to get a boat off the island. But the cottage where I'm staying is very nice. Old, but nice; so that's good, no need to worry. It's one of a very few on the island. It's cool and gray here most days, windy, these looming clouds. It feels so isolated. I really just mean that I feel lonely sometimes. But like I said, don't you worry. There are other people, a few. I see them sometimes. And a boat comes once a week, a big sturdy thing that seems to defy the waves. No passage though, as far as I can tell. Just practical things, it arrives with food and supplies, and of course there's the mail delivery. That's how I've been writing to you and I hope you're getting every letter. I enjoy writing them, so it passes the time. But mostly I sit on the hill nearby thinking of you both, hoping you are well and waiting for some news. If you have time, please, I would love to hear how you are doing. I miss you more than you can possibly know.

With all love…

(The **YOUNG MAN** *is knocked from his reverie by the sound of footsteps approaching. A man enters carrying a worn leather satchel over his shoulder, the strap crossing his chest, a worn hat.)*

POSTMAN. Anything to post today?

YOUNG MAN. No deliveries?

POSTMAN. No deliveries.

YOUNG MAN. No word at all?

POSTMAN. Nope, I'm afraid nothing today.

(The **YOUNG MAN** *takes it in, folds the letter and seals it inside the envelope.)*

YOUNG MAN. All right then. Can you send this for me?

(The **POSTMAN** *takes the letter.)*

POSTMAN. Saw all those black birds outside.

YOUNG MAN. They've been following me.

POSTMAN. Have they? Well, they sure do seem to like your little cottage.

YOUNG MAN. I've never seen birds that big anywhere, with those long necks. I don't know. Where I grew up, on the beach, it was so different than this. I've never seen such dull sand before. And the birds were nothing like these. They just sit there.

POSTMAN. Almost like they're waiting for something.

YOUNG MAN. It is a bit like that, now that you mention it. Odd.

POSTMAN. Well, I don't know how much longer you're staying, but I'd suggest shooing them away every once in a while. Don't want them to get too comfortable.

YOUNG MAN. Oh, I know.

POSTMAN. Because it's already been quite some time.

YOUNG MAN. Doesn't feel like that long.

POSTMAN. Guess not.

YOUNG MAN. Doesn't matter, I'm not planning on staying much longer.

POSTMAN. Oh no?

YOUNG MAN. No. I need to get home. It's taking a while, but I'll get there.

POSTMAN. Hope you do, sir. I'll be sure this gets out today.

YOUNG MAN. Thanks.

(The **POSTMAN** *begins to exit. He stops next to the pile, pulls out the envelope, tears it up and drops the pieces onto the mass of shredded paper. He exits.)*

(The **YOUNG MAN** *is left gazing out the window.)*

END SCENE

ii. requiem

(A small clearing amongst a group of bare birch trees.)

*(**CONNOR** sits on the ground. He is still in his pants from earlier and still shirtless, but he is now barefoot and blindfolded with a white strip of fabric. He is also soaking wet.)*

*(Next to him, an immense **BLACK BIRD** stands grooming itself. After a moment, it looks over thoughtfully.)*

BLACK BIRD. How are you feeling?

CONNOR. Still weak.

BLACK BIRD. Yes. Yes.

CONNOR. I wish I could see you.

BLACK BIRD. It's better if you don't.

CONNOR. I want to see you.

BLACK BIRD. Yes. As is the case with most things, and especially this thing, what you want might not be the very best thing.

CONNOR. And what is this thing?

BLACK BIRD. What are you doing here now?

CONNOR. I'm waiting for my wife, Danielle, and I want to know what's going on?

BLACK BIRD. Yes. Well then, we're waiting.

CONNOR. I want to take off this blindfold.

BLACK BIRD. It doesn't come off.

CONNOR. What does that mean?

BLACK BIRD. If you could manage to get it off, which you won't, it wouldn't make a difference, so best you leave it alone.

CONNOR. That doesn't make [any...]

BLACK BIRD. [What are] you doing here now?

CONNOR. I'm, I just said I'm waiting for my wife.

BLACK BIRD. Just your wife?

CONNOR. Who else would be here?

BLACK BIRD. Yes. That's right. Can you feel the chill in the air? I'm sure if I can feel it, with all of these feathers, then you must feel it.

CONNOR. Feathers?

BLACK BIRD. Ah yes, so many feathers.

CONNOR. Can you help me?

BLACK BIRD. Can you rise yet?

(CONNOR makes a feeble attempt to stand, but fails.)

CONNOR. Damn it.

BLACK BIRD. I'm here to help.

CONNOR. Then give me your hand and help me.

BLACK BIRD. Yes. Not like that.

CONNOR. Well, then what good [are you?]

BLACK BIRD. [What are] you doing here now?

CONNOR. I'm waiting for my wife. Stop asking me that.

BLACK BIRD. Yes.

(Pause. The BLACK BIRD goes back to grooming itself.)

CONNOR. Are you, are you still there?

BLACK BIRD. Yes.

CONNOR. I think it's getting colder.

BLACK BIRD. Yes?

CONNOR. I can feel it on my skin.

BLACK BIRD. And how does that feel?

(pause)

If you don't want to talk to me, I can leave.

CONNOR. No, don't.

BLACK BIRD. Ah, don't want to be alone.

CONNOR. I can't see anything.

BLACK BIRD. And it's very cold.

CONNOR. Yes.

BLACK BIRD. Yes. How does it feel on your skin? If you tell me, things will start to get easier.

CONNOR. It feels…it makes my skin tighten. That's not the right way to, my body braces against it from the inside out. From the inside to the outside I feel every little ripple of every little gust of every little breath of every little sigh she makes through the water sinking into the water everywhere and there's nothing I can do in that sigh in that breath with my hand that won't reach her every, no. No.

BLACK BIRD. Tell me.

CONNOR. I won't. This is, this is…

(He tries to rise again and falls to the ground again.)

BLACK BIRD. I'm sure, if you summon all of the strength you have left, you could drag yourself in whatever direction you hope to walk. But what direction is that? Where would you go if you could go and you can't go so you won't go so do try to rest, all right?

CONNOR. Why won't you fucking help me?

BLACK BIRD. This is helping.

CONNOR. Ugh.

BLACK BIRD. Yes. What are you doing here now?

CONNOR. I'm waiting for…I can't remember.

BLACK BIRD. Yes.

CONNOR. Why can't I remember?

*(Snow begins to fall in the clearing. The **BLACK BIRD** ruffles its feathers a bit and looks up to the sky.)*

BLACK BIRD. Ah look, it's beginning to snow.

END SCENE

iii. ghost story

(An intimate teahouse.)

(The **SEAMSTRESS** *sits on a cushion in something that might be a dressing gown and a robe, all very simple. Her complexion is quite pale. She is embroidering some kind of fabric remnant while humming.)*

(The **PROPRIETRESS** *is at a small table covered with different kettles and cups preparing tea. She looks vaguely Victorian in dress, structured and layered but crisper, simpler. No frills.)*

(The sound of waves can be heard from outside.)

*(***DANIELLE** *stands, soaking wet, in the doorway. She is barefoot and in a dark undershirt as she now carries her wet oversized sweater.)*

PROPRIETRESS. Oh, come in dear, you should come in before you catch your death.

(The **SEAMSTRESS** *laughs sharply and then continues humming.)*

Come on then, don't be shy.

DANIELLE. Thank you.

PROPRIETRESS. Here, let me get you a blanket.

(She grabs a folded up blanket from a stack next to the **SEAMSTRESS**.*)*

Are you going to say hello?

SEAMSTRESS. No.

PROPRIETRESS. Fine. Be impolite.

(She hands the blanket to **DANIELLE**.*)*

DANIELLE. Thank you.

PROPRIETRESS. Come sit down, you're drenched to the bone, aren't you? I'll just finish up the tea, that'll be the thing I'm sure.

DANIELLE. I saw your lamp in the window; I've been walking along the beach for so long.

PROPRIETRESS. Really now? Maybe an hour?

SEAMSTRESS. No.

PROPRIETRESS. A day?

SEAMSTRESS. No.

PROPRIETRESS. Oh, just listen to me. I'm sure it wasn't that long. Here, take this.

(*She passes a warm cup of tea to* **DANIELLE**.)

DANIELLE. It's so warm.

PROPRIETRESS. Not too warm though, just enough. You'll see. [Taste it.]

SEAMSTRESS. [Taste it.]

DANIELLE. What kind is it?

PROPRIETRESS. What kind do you think? Hmm?

(*The* **SEAMSTRESS** *begins laughing again.*)

You'll find that there are any number of ways through this little chat we're about to have and that questions, all of your questions, will only make it harder.

DANIELLE. What do you mean?

PROPRIETRESS. Harder.

DANIELLE. I'm only asking [what...]

PROPRIETRESS. [Harder,] harder, harder.

(*Pause. The women stare at her.* **DANIELLE** *sips the tea.*)

DANIELLE. Lavender.

PROPRIETRESS. Yes.

DANIELLE. It's very good.

PROPRIETRESS. Thank you. Now then, isn't that nicer? Oh, do you need something to eat?

DANIELLE. No. No thank you.

PROPRIETRESS. Well then, I'll just fix a cup for myself and then we'll chat.

(*The* **PROPRIETRESS** *begins pouring water from one pot to another and then one pot to another, and another, with no order, there's something rhythmic about it, something methodical, something natural and graceful.*)

DANIELLE. This is, this is a lovely little teahouse.

SEAMSTRESS. No.

PROPRIETRESS. Why thank you, dear.

SEAMSTRESS. No.

PROPRIETRESS. Just ignore her, if you can. I do try to keep it up, or at least, I do my best. There are so many little details, more than you could imagine. More than you'd ever even consider just by looking. And so many tiny things are happening all the time that it can feel a little overwhelming. Now…

(She stops pouring. She picks up a cup and sips it, taking in **DANIELLE**.*)*

(awkward pause)

DANIELLE. You said, you mentioned we would chat.

PROPRIETRESS. Mmm, yes. I did indeed, yes, but I thought you might start as you seem to have an awfully urgent need to share your feelings with me.

DANIELLE. What do [you…?]

PROPRIETRESS. [Ah, ah,] that sounds like a question.

DANIELLE. All right then; I don't know what you mean.

PROPRIETRESS. *(with a laugh)* She doesn't know what I mean.

SEAMSTRESS. No.

PROPRIETRESS. Maybe the cold water gave you a bit of a shock?

SEAMSTRESS. No.

PROPRIETRESS. Hmm, well, you have nothing but time to decipher my meaning. And I certainly have more time than I know what to do with, so please do take your time.

(Pause. The **PROPRIETRESS** *returns to pouring the water, one pot to the next, to the next. The* **SEAMSTRESS** *begins to hum again as she sews and sews.)*

DANIELLE. I think I know that song.

PROPRIETRESS. Wouldn't be surprised at all.

DANIELLE. I can't quite place it.

PROPRIETRESS. Probably best you don't. Just drink your
tea.

DANIELLE. I'm almost certain I've heard that tune before.

(The SEAMSTRESS *chuckles and gently sets down her
sewing.)*

SEAMSTRESS. [Only song I know.]

PROPRIETRESS. [Only song I know.]

DANIELLE. Is it?

PROPRIETRESS. Questions.

SEAMSTRESS. You know, my hands are aching; they ache,
they feel stiff. Like maple trees. No, nothing so lush;
more like birch under the skin, in the skin. Can you
hear them? My fingers crack with the sound of breaking branches. Fingers much older than I could ever
be; I don't look old, do I? You might call it a generosity
of this place.

(She leans forward.)

Deceptive. But this cracking in my fingers, it doesn't
hurt. Or it hurts less than remembering everything
before, you know? It takes the place of memory, sweet
and crisp, and then it's not even me anymore; it hasn't
been me for a long time. Some other hands, some
fashioned things. They move almost as if they have
their own strange will.

*(She examines her hands as if they were some strange
new things.)*

A long time ago, these hands belonged to another
woman, a strong and beautiful woman. And she lost
her child, as you did.

DANIELLE. No. Did I?

PROPRIETRESS. Finish your [tea.]

DANIELLE. [Lost] a child.

PROPRIETRESS. An accident, plain and [simple.]

SEAMSTRESS. [And she] blamed the ocean, as you did.

DANIELLE. The ocean.

PROPRIETRESS. There are just so [many details.]

SEAMSTRESS. [And she] wished for everything to go away, as you did.

DANIELLE. I didn't do that.

SEAMSTRESS. You did. As she did. She wished it in a fit of anguish and fear, weeping into the water. She screamed and wailed through her tears until every vein in her throat coalesced into coarse knots of rope and the skies grew dark, the wind grew fierce, the waves listened and came alive. She stood and faced a great wave as it crashed down on her with a deafening roar. You know that sound. The sound of water so ferocious that it rends buildings, fells the oldest trees, just imagine what it did to her flesh and bone. You know that too. But her scream, that mix of unbearable sorrow and rage, it clung to the waves, with hands, these hands that never tire no matter how sore, no matter how much pain.

(The **PROPRIETRESS** *stops pouring and turns her attention to the* **SEAMSTRESS**. **DANIELLE***'s eyes come alive while the* **SEAMSTRESS** *speaks, she sees the* **PROPRIETRESS***; she begins to identify her.)*

How could the ocean ever know that it would never be free of that grief it [swallowed?]

PROPRIETRESS. [That's] enough.

SEAMSTRESS. It's still here between the waves and it comes to its kind, it finds its [like, it…]

PROPRIETRESS. [I said] that's enough, I don't like this story, I don't like the unpleasant task of having to hear it over and over again. Even if I don't listen, I still hear it.

(The **SEAMSTRESS** *picks up her sewing and begins humming again.)*

Now, would you like some more tea?

DANIELLE. No, I haven't finished and I think I...

(**DANIELLE** *slowly points at the* **PROPRIETRESS**.)

PROPRIETRESS. What is it, dear?

DANIELLE. I think I know you.

SEAMSTRESS. *(in a sing-song voice with a laugh)* [Noooooo.]

PROPRIETRESS. [No you don't.]

DANIELLE. Yes, I know you.

PROPRIETRESS. If you insist, then you must think you do. But thinking you do and actually knowing, well those are two very different things. But just look at your face, you're convinced and that's that.

DANIELLE. Monster.

PROPRIETRESS. So now, it would seem, you're ready for our chat. Just let me finish [my tea.]

DANIELLE. [You. You] took my son.

PROPRIETRESS. Do sit down. This might take a few minutes.

SEAMSTRESS. Give or take.

(The **PROPRIETRESS** *sips her tea.)*

DANIELLE. You fucking took my son.

PROPRIETRESS. This doesn't have to [be as...]

DANIELLE. [Shut your] mouth! How can you sit there so calmly, offering me tea, acting like you're not a thief, a vicious thief? We lived next to you, moved to be near you, thought you were beautiful, let you in our lives, trusted [you.]

(The **PROPRIETRESS** *rises.)*

PROPRIETRESS. [Let me] [in your lives?]

DANIELLE. [Trusted you!] And you took him, dragged him away from us, from me, into the water, into the, is he, is he here? Do you have him here [somewhere?]

PROPRIETRESS. [Are you] hearing this?

(The **SEAMSTRESS** *laughs.)*

SEAMSTRESS. No.

DANIELLE. Are you hiding him, holding him [here?]

SEAMSTRESS. [Look] around and tell me, where would he be?

DANIELLE. I want him back, you awful [woman!]

PROPRIETRESS. [I've given] you shelter, something warm to drink, something dry. You saw my lamp and came in out of the cold. I'm a haven to you in the storm and I'm awful? I sent you all of those fish to appease you, left them right there on the beach, and I'm awful? I've brought you here, to me, and [I'm awful?]

DANIELLE. [Do you] think anything else you could give me, anything else you could do, would make up for what you've stolen? I only want to [find him.]

PROPRIETRESS. [Are you] under the impression that I'm trying to make up for something? Do you think you're here because I'm particularly interested in hearing your bile, this indiscriminate venom? Perhaps I've tried to explain, perhaps I've tried to mollify, in my way, but if you think I'm sorry then you're sorely mistaken.

(The **PROPRIETRESS** *spins on her heel.)*

DANIELLE. I'm not done with you, not by any [stretch of…]

PROPRIETRESS. [No you're] not.

DANIELLE. I fucking hate you.

PROPRIETRESS. You've made that more than [clear.]

SEAMSTRESS. [Can you] feel that?

PROPRIETRESS. *(turning sharply on the* **SEAMSTRESS***)* You be quiet.

SEAMSTRESS. I can feel [it.]

DANIELLE. [I think] you're cruel. Cruel! I think [you're…]

PROPRIETRESS. [Oh, is that] what you think?

(She picks up a cup from the table.)

DANIELLE. Yes!

PROPRIETRESS. Well I'm so glad!

(She smashes the cup on the ground.)

Thank you!

(She smashes a teapot to the ground.)

Oh how telling! Thank you!

(The **PROPRIETRESS** *continues picking up cups and teapots full of water and throwing them at the ground pointedly in a whirlwind of ferocity, causing* **DANIELLE** *to back away. The* **SEAMSTRESS** *begins cackling with delight at the outburst and her laughter only grows more manic…)*

You think you're important enough to warrant some malicious scheme?! Some dark awful thing that I plotted and planned?! I do hope you know how much time I spend worried about you, specifically, individually, in the midst of everything else I do or do you imagine, do you ever let the thought creep into the cracks of those angry, crumbling walls inside your brain that maybe I didn't even notice your son, maybe he's so inconceivably minute to me in the much larger scope of things, and I have a much larger scope I assure you, that I didn't even notice him because it's not my job to notice him, I'm not his mother and I do not cry over things that are accidents, accidents, or things that just happen, like tides, like tears, like your son caught in my wake. So much easier to hate me.

(The **PROPRIETRESS** *regroups a bit, but the* **SEAMSTRESS** *is racked with delight as* **DANIELLE** *finally breaks down, collapsing, coming completely undone.)*

DANIELLE. He was just standing there and then he was gone. He was there and then gone. There wasn't any kind of warning, there [wasn't any…]

PROPRIETRESS. [When you] realize that your grief has brought you here; you'll regret it. This won't be the great reckoning you hoped for, not by any stretch of the imagination. You can't reckon with me, how could you? Hear this, you hear this: you will never find what you've come here to find and you'd best begin accepting that simple truth.

(Pause. **DANIELLE** *is weeping. The* **PROPRIETRESS** *smoothes herself out.)*

Now do your best to calm down. Oh, just look at this mess.

(The **PROPRIETRESS** *begins collecting the pieces of broken cups and pots. After a moment…)*

DANIELLE. I don't, I don't know what to do.

(The **SEAMSTRESS** *laughs at* **DANIELLE**.*)*

PROPRIETRESS. You're crying now. That's something.

END SCENE

iv. epistolary

(The cottage. It is darker outside now.)

(The **YOUNG MAN** *stands alone. He holds a piece of paper in one hand and an envelope in the other. He still has an air of optimism.)*

(The single straight-back chair has been tipped over.)

(The adjacent pile of shredded paper, torn-up envelopes and unsent mail has grown larger in size.)

YOUNG MAN. Dear Mom and Dad,

I miss you and I know, trust me, I know I've been gone for a long time, whatever that means, but I hope you're not too upset. Sorry to say that it seems I'll be delayed. Again. It's not funny, but it makes me laugh. I wish I could explain it to you, or understand myself. I wait every day, but to no avail. And no word from you, that's hard, but I would love to hear from you. I'm not exactly sure how many letters I've sent now, but yes, absolutely, I would love to hear any news from you. Will you please send me something, anything that reminds me of home? This place, the place where I am, it's so different. In fact, the more I, the closer I look, the more everything here is somehow off. Just a bit. Like the time you took me to see that silly cartoon movie where the sound didn't match up with the picture. Do you remember that? That's the kind of place where I am. But nothing here has changed much since the last letter. I think it might be grayer, but of course that's just my imagination. And if you can believe it, there appear to be even fewer people than I had first thought. I hope I'll hear from you soon. Do you miss me? I want to come home, you have to believe me, and I will, I will see this thing out. I've come too far already to give up now. I'll find some kind of passage soon. I promise, you'll see.

With all love…

(The sound of footsteps causes the **YOUNG MAN**'s head *to jerk up. The* **POSTMAN** *enters again carrying the same small cloth bag over his shoulder, the strap crossing his chest.)*

POSTMAN. Anything to post today?

YOUNG MAN. No deliveries.

POSTMAN. No.

YOUNG MAN. No word.

POSTMAN. No.

(The **YOUNG MAN** *takes it in, then folds the letter and seals it inside the envelope.)*

YOUNG MAN. All right then. Can you send this for me?

(The **POSTMAN** *takes the letter.)*

POSTMAN. It's, I don't mean to speak out of turn, but it's kind of a mess in here, huh?

YOUNG MAN. I can't bring myself to clean it up.

POSTMAN. Oh.

YOUNG MAN. It's the birds.

POSTMAN. You, uh, you let those birds start coming inside?

YOUNG MAN. I wouldn't say I "let them." They just started coming inside. I can't keep them out. I lock the door and close up the windows, but they're smart, they come right in. Only at night though, during the day the just sit out there.

POSTMAN. Ah.

YOUNG MAN. Every time I clean up, they're back in here again.

POSTMAN. They're persistent. And they'll eat you out of house and home if you let 'em.

YOUNG MAN. They eat everything. They even peck at me in my sleep, at my head and face. And they're so big.

POSTMAN. You know, I'm not sure they're particularly large. But to be fair, I've only ever seen these birds so I could be mistaken.

YOUNG MAN. Doesn't matter, I'm not afraid of some birds.

POSTMAN. Oh no?

YOUNG MAN. I'm not afraid of much. I know how that sounds, but, well, it's the truth. When I was a little kid, so young that it's hard to remember, there was an accident. I almost drowned. I don't know how long I was in the ocean, but I washed up far away. So far away.

POSTMAN. And so young.

YOUNG MAN. But I took care of myself. I still don't know how, and it's taken a long time, but I'm almost back. I can feel it.

POSTMAN. Must be hard to tell though.

YOUNG MAN. What?

POSTMAN. Oh, nothing really, it's just that you don't know where you are, where you were. Must be hard to tell is all.

YOUNG MAN. I don't care; I won't give up.

(He breaks away from the **POSTMAN** *and returns to his corner. He sets the chair upright and sits down.)*

POSTMAN. Sorry, didn't mean to upset you.

YOUNG MAN. No, I just need to get some sleep.

POSTMAN. Ah, that I understand. It's been so long since I got any sleep, I find it hard to remember sleeping at all. These birds, they keep me awake when I think I might be tired, something like tired, but that honestly doesn't happen very much anymore. It often feels to me, walking up to one of these doors or tying off a knot in the rope at the dock, like some kind of waking dream. The repetitive motion of it all, I mean. Doing work on my boat, even though it's well made, well cared for and doesn't need much work. Sailing from here to there, cutting through waves that aren't as welcoming as memory tells me they once were to do business that isn't as heartening as it seems it once was. And letter upon letter. Every bit of it has a lilting quality; it all fades. Continuously, you understand, like everything here has always been fading.

(He holds up the letter and examines it.)

Huh, and then I think how fanciful that all sounds and it vanishes. Just like that, because I've got work to do. When it comes down to it, those kinds of reveries, I'll tell you, can be such a distraction from accomplishing task at hand.

(The **POSTMAN** *nods, a moment of acknowledgment.)*

YOUNG MAN. Huh. You know, no one has talked to me this much here. Maybe ever.

POSTMAN. I should get moving.

YOUNG MAN. Oh.

POSTMAN. Try your best not to worry about the birds.

YOUNG MAN. You said they'll eat me out of house and home.

POSTMAN. Yes, they will.

YOUNG MAN. I guess I don't really have much left.

POSTMAN. I'll be sure this gets out today.

YOUNG MAN. Okay. Thanks.

(The **POSTMAN** *begins to exit. He stops next to the pile, pulls out the envelope, looks over his shoulder at the* **YOUNG MAN***, tears it up and drops the pieces onto the mass of shredded paper. He exits.)*

END SCENE

v. requiem

(The small clearing amongst a group of bare birch trees.)

*(**CONNOR** still sits on the ground blindfolded.)*

*(The **BLACK BIRD** bobs its head a bit in the falling snow. After a moment, the bird shakes out its wings, knocking the accumulation of snow from its feathers.)*

BLACK BIRD. The snow is beautiful.

CONNOR. I can't see it.

BLACK BIRD. So gentle, I never get used to it.

CONNOR. It's so cold.

BLACK BIRD. Yes. You said; you started to say. It must seem cold, but trust that it's not entirely true. For you. There is still warmth. There is still something other than this.

CONNOR. Is it near here? The place you're talking about, can we go there?

BLACK BIRD. Yes. It's not a place.

CONNOR. Can we go anywhere? Please, anywhere?

BLACK BIRD. Can you rise yet?

CONNOR. You know I can't.

BLACK BIRD. Then for now we're here. And the air is cold. And the snow is soft as it disappears.

*(As he speaks, **CONNOR** holds out his hand, catching some of the snow.)*

CONNOR. It melts.

BLACK BIRD. Yes, it disappears.

CONNOR. I can feel it on my hand.

*(The **BLACK BIRD** darts out its head on its long slender neck, its beak very close.)*

BLACK BIRD. Tell me.

CONNOR. No.

BLACK BIRD. Tell me.

CONNOR. No.

BLACK BIRD. The snow is falling in your hand.

CONNOR. No.

BLACK BIRD. Yes, it is. You can feel it.

CONNOR. I can feel it.

BLACK BIRD. Disappearing.

CONNOR. Melting.

BLACK BIRD. Tell me.

(As **CONNOR** *speaks, the bird looks upward and stretches its wings out to their full length, filled up by torrent of memory and perception flooding out.)*

CONNOR. The snow lands on my palm, it touches me and immediately it becomes something else, sliding down my hand, lighting up my skin. It's cold, cool, then wet and then something else, like everything it becomes something else as soon as you feel it, something else that you can't have in your hand, something else that's gone away, a hand slipping from my grip, trying to pull, fingers slipping from my fingers slipping through the water and her eyes and her hair and her hand, but smaller now, a smaller hand, a child's hand, my hand in my father's hand, his eyes, filling his eyes, and my mother's arm around us, my hand in my father's, and then my son's in mine, no, no, no, that I didn't hold, two hands, one hand, two hands slipping, fingers slipping and my mouth full of water and lungs full of water like this, like the snow falling, but faster, kissing her, promises, wet promises and more and more and more, so much that I can't find air, it can't get in and it can't get out and my chest feels like it might explode or collapse or tear open because there's nothing left, nothing left but white, bright something cracking, light, out of my chest and spilling her out with my blood on her fingers from the scratch on my chest and then her fingers on my chest, gentle, and then her fingers in my fingers slipping away with the clean furniture, everything clean, everything wet, everything crushed, everything cleansed of her, of me, of her, of us, of her, of him, no, no, no, it slips through my fingers like water, like sand, like beautiful creations spiraling out of a young boy's imagination, the water takes them, build them, take them, build them, so much grander, more beautiful than they ever could have, it's the love that makes me, in my head, see them, larger than they ever, more to lose, immense and crumbling, the water takes everything, them, her, me , him, everything, nothing permanent, every single thing slides away, down my hand, then it's cold, then it's now and I only have the one thing, the one thing for him, the one thing I have to keep….

*(The **BLACK BIRD** lets out a loud cry, something deafening that echoes through the space. It startles **CONNOR** causing him to pull away. But in the effort, he collapses to the ground, worked into a state, shaking, out of breath.)*

BLACK BIRD. Don't be afraid. How do you feel? Won't you talk to me? Ah, won't open your mouth? There's something else, one more thing? You have to let it escape.

CONNOR. That's everything.

BLACK BIRD. You have to let it go.

CONNOR. There's nothing else.

BLACK BIRD. Yes, something, a letter?

CONNOR. I said there's nothing else.

BLACK BIRD. A letter.

CONNOR. No.

BLACK BIRD. A son.

CONNOR. I won't.

BLACK BIRD. Yes, there is one more thing to release and you haven't but you will as you should, you will and then you'll be able to rise. So close, so close. But you've already given so much to carry, even for me. So I must be on my way.

CONNOR. Please don't leave.

BLACK BIRD. If you do not let go of that one, last thing, I will come back with others. I will come back with others and we…we will have to take it from you. I am sorry; that is our work. But if you release it, well, then you will suddenly see. Everything.

CONNOR. I can't see anything, don't leave me alone.

(The **BLACK BIRD** *flaps out its wings a bit, stretching them.)*

BLACK BIRD. Yes. Everything.

(Blackout into the sounds of wings flapping as the **BLACK BIRD** *flies away.)*

END SCENE

vi. epistolary

(The **YOUNG MAN** *sits alone on the floor of the cottage, backed into a corner. His hands are over his face. It is now even darker outside.)*

(The adjacent pile of shredded paper, torn up envelopes and unsent mail is still present and has been scattered about.)

(The sound of footsteps as the **POSTMAN** *enters again carrying his small cloth bag over his shoulder, the strap crossing his chest.)*

POSTMAN. Anything to…

(He takes in the room and deflates a bit. He's later than he intended.)

Anything to post today?

YOUNG MAN. No.

POSTMAN. No letter?

YOUNG MAN. I can't, I can't write letters anymore. Those birds pecked out my eyes. There were too many of them, I couldn't stop it and they just came in here in the dark and…

(The **POSTMAN** *crosses, reaches into his bag and produces a long, thin piece of white cloth. He hands it to the* **YOUNG MAN.***)*

POSTMAN. Take this. Here you go, take it.

(The **YOUNG MAN** *takes the cloth tentatively and, after a moment, wraps it around his head, covering his eyes. He faces out.)*

YOUNG MAN. Thank you.

POSTMAN. Saw them on the way in. The birds. There are even more now, all over the eave of your roof, the lawn outside.

YOUNG MAN. They come and go as they please. There's nothing I can do now. And I can't leave yet. I have to wait here until I can find some way to move on.

POSTMAN. Well, this may be small comfort after everything you've been through…but you have a letter.

YOUNG MAN. A letter for me?

POSTMAN. Must be for you, there's no one else left here.

(The **POSTMAN** *produces a letter from his bag and puts it in the* **YOUNG MAN***'s hands. He turns it over and over like something completely foreign and new.)*

YOUNG MAN. Everyone else is gone?

POSTMAN. There's no one else.

YOUNG MAN. Can you, will you read it to me?

(The **POSTMAN** *takes the letter back, tears it open and begins reading…)*

POSTMAN. Dear…there's, I can't make out the name. It's smudged.

YOUNG MAN. I can't remember my name, just keep going.

POSTMAN. All right then…

(The **POSTMAN** *looks over his shoulder and gestures out. Lights rise on the clearing amongst the birch trees. Snow continues to fall on a blindfolded* **CONNOR**. *He sits broken and empty. The bird has gone.)*

CONNOR. I'm not sure why I'm writing this, not sure what to say. I almost feel like I should try to draw you a picture, something sweet, or just tear a page out of one of your storybooks instead of trying to say, I don't know, I wish I could give you something you'd enjoy. Anything. But I can't make up for how we let you down. And I know I shouldn't think of it that way, but I do. I do. Now that you're gone, now that…you're dead, there's no "I'm sorry" that could ever begin to make things right. And because you're out there in the water, not here, out there, this is the best I can do. I've never been, I know it's hard to hear your Daddy say these things, but I've never been religious. Do you know what that means? It means a lot of things really, especially now. But mostly, I've never been the kind of man that believes in Heaven. But everything in me needs to believe that if you had to be taken away, if you had to go so young, that you're in Heaven now, whatever that means, that you're safe, and well cared for, and somewhere that makes more sense than this, than being here without you. And if I can believe that...I have to believe it, I have to help your mom, when she's ready, believe it too. And I have to let you go. But I will always love you. Know that, you know that. You're my little guy and I...

(He breaks up a bit, but pulls it together.)

Your mom and I both, we will love you. Always. Goodbye.

Dad

(The snow continues to fall. The **YOUNG MAN** *is weeping and cannot hide it. The* **POSTMAN** *slowly lowers the later.)*

YOUNG MAN. Is that all?

POSTMAN. That's all.

YOUNG MAN. I don't, so I should...I should keep waiting then. Here? With these awful birds? I don't even know what for now, what am I waiting for?

POSTMAN. If you can, just let the birds do their work.

YOUNG MAN. I can't stop them.

POSTMAN. No, you can't.

YOUNG MAN. Can you at least tell me where I am?

POSTMAN. I don't... It'd be hard to say.

YOUNG MAN. Hard to say?

POSTMAN. Hard to explain. To you.

YOUNG MAN. But, I don't, but...clearly it's not heaven.

POSTMAN. I hope not, sir.

(He hands the letter back to the **YOUNG MAN** *and exits.)*

(After a moment, the **YOUNG MAN** *tears up the letter and lets the pieces fall to the ground, mixing with the other scraps, an echo of the falling snow.)*

(Light floods down on the **YOUNG MAN** *and* **CONNOR**, *both now blindfolded. They tilt their heads up into the light, towards the heavens. They begin to rise from their knees, pulled up by the light, filled with a yearning to ascend that cannot be denied. The lights grow even brighter and the sound of birds calling, wings flapping, hundreds of wings. It grows cacophonous.)*

(blackout)

END SCENE

vii. ghost story

*(The teahouse. **DANIELLE** and the **SEAMSTRESS** are in the exact same spots. The **SEAMSTRESS** hums her tune, sewing away.)*

*(After a moment, the **PROPRIETRESS** enters from the storm outside. She is holding a large antique looking umbrella and carrying a bundle of wet letters bound with twine.)*

(She sets down the bundle on the table and begins shaking out her umbrella.)

PROPRIETRESS. It's really something out there. I just love when the weather gets tumultuous. Oh look, you're still here?

DANIELLE. The storm's so intense.

PROPRIETRESS. Quite right. I barely even made it to the post box.

DANIELLE. It doesn't seem safe.

PROPRIETRESS. Of course not, and where would you go? Now, you've had a little rest and did you two get to spend some time together?

SEAMSTRESS. No.

PROPRIETRESS. Ah, well, plenty of time for that I suppose.

*(The **SEAMSTRESS** laughs.)*

DANIELLE. I'd like to go and find my husband now.

PROPRIETRESS. I'm sorry?

DANIELLE. Maybe he found someplace like this, [but I...]

PROPRIETRESS. [Someplace] like this?

DANIELLE. He might be alone or he [might...]

PROPRIETRESS. [You won't] find him.

DANIELLE. I'd like to go, I'd like to leave.

PROPRIETRESS. You can't ever leave.

DANIELLE.What?

PROPRIETRESS. [No.]

SEAMSTRESS. [No.]

DANIELLE. I need to find him.

(She rises to leave.)

PROPRIETRESS. Your husband or your son?

DANIELLE. Don't you ever talk about my son; I'm leaving now.

PROPRIETRESS. I wouldn't.

*(**DANIELLE** opens the front door. A deafening roar of waves, wind and people's voices in harshly amplified whispers; a flood of sounds streaming past the door that knocks her back. She forces the door closed and leans against it.)*

PROPRIETRESS. More tea?

DANIELLE. What is that?

PROPRIETRESS. Ah, memories of so many lifetimes being stripped away.

DANIELLE. I don't, where are we?

PROPRIETRESS. Not the same place where you first arrived, certainly. Everything's always moving, Danielle.

DANIELLE. Yes, yes that's my name.

SEAMSTRESS. No.

PROPRIETRESS. Yes it was.

DANIELLE. Danielle.

PROPRIETRESS. Don't worry, you'll forget it soon enough.

*(The **SEAMSTRESS** giggles.)*

DANIELLE. What else do you want, what can you possibly take, there's nothing [left to…]

PROPRIETRESS. [Now I've had] some time to compose myself, but don't think that I won't get angry [again.]

DANIELLE. [Please, just] tell me what you want.

*(The **PROPRIETRESS** places a hand on **DANIELLE**'s shoulder, causing her to flinch away. The **PROPRIETRESS** gently touches her face.)*

PROPRIETRESS. I want some peace. I want to go about my business as I did for longer than memory exists, before...

(The SEAMSTRESS *laughs, mocking. The* PROPRIETRESS *turns to looks at her.)*

Well, we never really know how very wrong we can be, isn't that right? [I should have known better.]

SEAMSTRESS. [I should have known better.]

(The PROPRIETRESS *returns to her table.)*

DANIELLE. You should have known what?

PROPRIETRESS. As you said, the same motions over and over again. I don't know why, [I simply can't seem to help myself.]

SEAMSTRESS. [I simply can't seem to help myself.]

DANIELLE. I'm here because of her?

(The SEAMSTRESS *laughs again, shaking her head.)*

PROPRIETRESS. You're here because of you. And your incessant questioning is [interminable.]

SEAMSTRESS. [Do you] know I could hear you on the beach? Crying, screaming, I could hear you and not just hear you, but feel you; I can still feel you. Between here and there, I can feel you there and here and all around. And I'm so lonely.

PROPRIETRESS. And noisy.

SEAMSTRESS. I didn't ask to come here.

PROPRIETRESS. A matter of opinion.

SEAMSTRESS. *(quick and vicious)* No, no, it's not a matter of opinion, don't you listen to her and her pleasant voice and her shopkeeper tone, she's none of what you see. She's a thing.

PROPRIETRESS. I was trying to help you, weeping on the beach every day for a lost child. It's one of the very few times ever that I've been compelled to do something kind.

SEAMSTRESS. Killing me.

PROPRIETRESS. Releasing you.

SEAMSTRESS. Is that what you did?

PROPRIETRESS. That's what you asked for, didn't you? But you refuse to be released. I didn't know then that I'd be haunted by you forever. [Tormented.]

SEAMSTRESS. [Tormented.]

(The **SEAMSTRESS** *laughs again, a bitter, angry thing.)*

PROPRIETRESS. If you're so unhappy, then you can leave. Please, won't you leave? I've long since lost any interest in your company. You drive me near madness. Won't you just go? You can both go if you go together, how about that?

DANIELLE. I'll go.

PROPRIETRESS. Not unless you go together.

DANIELLE. Let's go, let's get out of here.

SEAMSTRESS. Where would I go? No, silly, I'm not going anywhere.

DANIELLE. She'll let us leave.

SEAMSTRESS. Maybe, maybe she can do that. But you don't know what that means. Better the devil you know.

PROPRIETRESS. I never should have invited [you in.]

SEAMSTRESS. [Invited?!]

PROPRIETRESS. And now I can't be rid [of you.]

SEAMSTRESS. [Just listen] to her; you'd think she'd actually know better. But she didn't and I didn't and now we're this. And I'd rather etiolate here, bleaching from lack of sunlight, brittle and sore and never [leaving.]

PROPRIETRESS. [And] never [leaving.]

SEAMSTRESS. [And] never [leaving.]

PROPRIETRESS. [And] never leaving.

DANIELLE. I'm not staying here.

SEAMSTRESS. Of course you are.

DANIELLE. I'm not like you.

SEAMSTRESS. Oh no? That's a very bold statement. All right, would you do me a favor? Would you just tell me your son's name?

PROPRIETRESS. There's no reason to be cruel.

SEAMSTRESS. I'm not being cruel; she says we're nothing alike, she says that, not me. Will you tell me your son's name?

DANIELLE. No.

SEAMSTRESS. You won't? Or you can't?

DANIELLE. I don't want to say it.

(As the SEAMSTRESS *speaks,* DANIELLE*'s breath becomes harder, even violent.)*

SEAMSTRESS. Do you feel that inside you now? When you think his name and can't make your mouth make the sounds that make it real? That's rage, that monstrous grief that won't let go of you, that sits in your stomach, kicking, demanding, and blunts your tongue and squeezes your lungs for every last bit of breath. You know what that is and you'd know by now if you were the kind of person who could ever let it go. And you're not.

DANIELLE. I'm not.

SEAMSTRESS. You're broken. And you're just like me.

(Suddenly DANIELLE*'s breath is caught in her throat and then all at once she falls apart. Her words have a similar effect on the* SEAMSTRESS; *her breath becomes more and more exaggerated as* DANIELLE *speaks.)*

DANIELLE. I don't know how to live without my son, I can't, no, without the way his face looked when he smiled, at me, at anything, the sound that he made when he used to see birds on the beach, that little involuntary noise, full of joy, eyes bright with wonder, warm, the way his hair smelled when I would kiss him goodnight, his hand on my cheek and how [he always…]

SEAMSTRESS. [Stop!]

(The SEAMSTRESS *cannot hear any more of it. Pause. After a moment…)*

DANIELLE. Everyone recovers, even if they never recover, I have to recover.

SEAMSTRESS. No, you don't. You really don't. You're already here; you've done the hardest part. Dying, the actual death, that's the most difficult part.

PROPRIETRESS. So lacking in any kind of grace.

DANIELLE. Death?

SEAMSTRESS. Your death.

DANIELLE. Mine.

SEAMSTRESS. Yours.

(*DANIELLE looks at her hands and goes pale. She slowly collapses into a sitting position on the floor still looking at her hands. She does not cry; it's almost as if she's been hollowed out. This lasts until...*)

DANIELLE. All of it, everything's gone?

PROPRIETRESS. Gone.

DANIELLE. The house and all [of the...?]

PROPRIETRESS. [Gone.]

DANIELLE. And Connor?

PROPRIETRESS. Gone.

DANIELLE. My...my son?

PROPRIETRESS. Everything but this.

SEAMSTRESS. So now you'll stay and be familiar, to me, here, keep me company.

PROPRIETRESS. Keep her quiet, keep her still.

SEAMSTRESS. And less alone.

DANIELLE. With each other.

SEAMSTRESS. Lonely together.

DANIELLE. Dead.

SEAMSTRESS. Only mostly. The sadness still has it's own kind of breath.

DANIELLE. And I don't have to live without him.

SEAMSTRESS. Because now you're here with me, like me.

DANIELLE. And I don't have to live without him.

SEAMSTRESS. Look at me.

(**DANIELLE** *finally looks at her.*)

I'm you.

DANIELLE. And never think of what we've lost.

SEAMSTRESS. And only think of what we've lost.

(*Pause.* **DANIELLE** *and the* **SEAMSTRESS** *stare at each other across the teahouse. The* **SEAMSTRESS** *reaches a hand, an invitation. It is genuine and full of longing. And then quietly…*)

DANIELLE. [Together.]

SEAMSTRESS. [Together.]

(*The* **PROPRIETRESS** *looks at the* **SEAMSTRESS** *and then to* **DANIELLE**.)

PROPRIETRESS. Good. Why don't you sit down dear, I'll get you some more tea.

(*The* **SEAMSTRESS** *sews and hums. The* **PROPRIETRESS** *sees the bundle of letters.*)

Oh, I nearly forgot. I'm unaccustomed to this commotion. Now, these will make you sad. There's no other way to say it. But they'll also give you a kind of, well, I don't know what they'll give you. They're from him. They're from your son.

(*She holds out the letters and* **DANIELLE** *snatches them away, clinging to them.*)

You'll see that they're not easy to read, but a lot of work went into piecing these thousands and thousands of scraps back together and I do hope you'll remember that. If I were you, I'd wait to start and read them slowly. It may seem like a good number of pages, but you have a very long time to fill.

DANIELLE. How long?

PROPRIETRESS. Read slowly.

(*The* **PROPRIETRESS** *smiles and returns to her table. She begins pouring and shifting pots again.* **DANIELLE** *fingers the twine knot holding the letters together. After a moment, she becomes aware of the* **SEAMSTRESS**' *song again, looking to her...)*

DANIELLE. What is that song?

(Pause. The **SEAMSTRESS** *stops and slowly looks directly at* **DANIELLE.***)*

SEAMSTRESS. A lullaby.

DANIELLE. It's agony.

SEAMSTRESS. [Yes.]

PROPRIETRESS. [Yes.]

(The **PROPRIETRESS** *continues pouring, the* **SEAMSTRESS** *continues humming as she resumes her sewing.* **DANIELLE** *sits quietly, handling letters from her son.)*

END OF PLAY

www.ingramcontent.com/pod-product-compliance
Lightning Source LLC
Chambersburg PA
CBHW070644120726
47909CB00004B/1575